Tom Brady
NFL Great and Super Bowl MVP

by Grace Hansen

Abdo
HISTORY MAKER
BIOGRAPHIES
Kids

abdobooks.com

Published by Abdo Kids, a division of ABDO, P.O. Box 398166, Minneapolis, Minnesota 55439.
Copyright © 2022 by Abdo Consulting Group, Inc. International copyrights reserved in all countries.
No part of this book may be reproduced in any form without written permission from the publisher.
Abdo Kids Jumbo™ is a trademark and logo of Abdo Kids.

Printed in the United States of America, North Mankato, Minnesota.

052021

092021

Photo Credits: Alamy, AP Images, Getty Images, Icon Sportswire, iStock, Shutterstock PREMIER

Production Contributors: Teddy Borth, Jennie Forsberg, Grace Hansen
Design Contributors: Candice Keimig, Pakou Moua

Library of Congress Control Number: 2021932485
Publisher's Cataloging-in-Publication Data

Names: Hansen, Grace, author.

Title: Tom Brady: NFL great and Super Bowl MVP / by Grace Hansen

Other title: NFL great and Super Bowl MVP

Description: Minneapolis, Minnesota : Abdo Kids, 2022 | Series: History maker biographies | Includes
    online resources and index.

Identifiers: ISBN 9781098208936 (lib. bdg.) | ISBN 9781098209070 (ebook) | ISBN 9781098209148
    (Read-to-Me ebook)

Subjects: LCSH: Brady, Tom, 1977---Juvenile literature. | Quarterbacks (Football)--United States--
    Biography--Juvenile literature. | Tampa Bay Buccaneers (Football team)--Juvenile literature. |
    Professional athletes--United States--Biography--Juvenile literature. | Super Bowl--Records--
    Juvenile literature.

Classification: DDC 796.332092--dc23

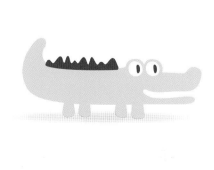

Table of Contents

Early Life & Education

Thomas Edward Patrick Brady Jr. was born on August 3, 1977. He grew up in San Mateo, California, with three older sisters.

California

Tom loved football from a young age. In high school, he was a star baseball and football player. After graduating in 1995, Tom was asked to play for a pro baseball team. But he said no. He had other plans.

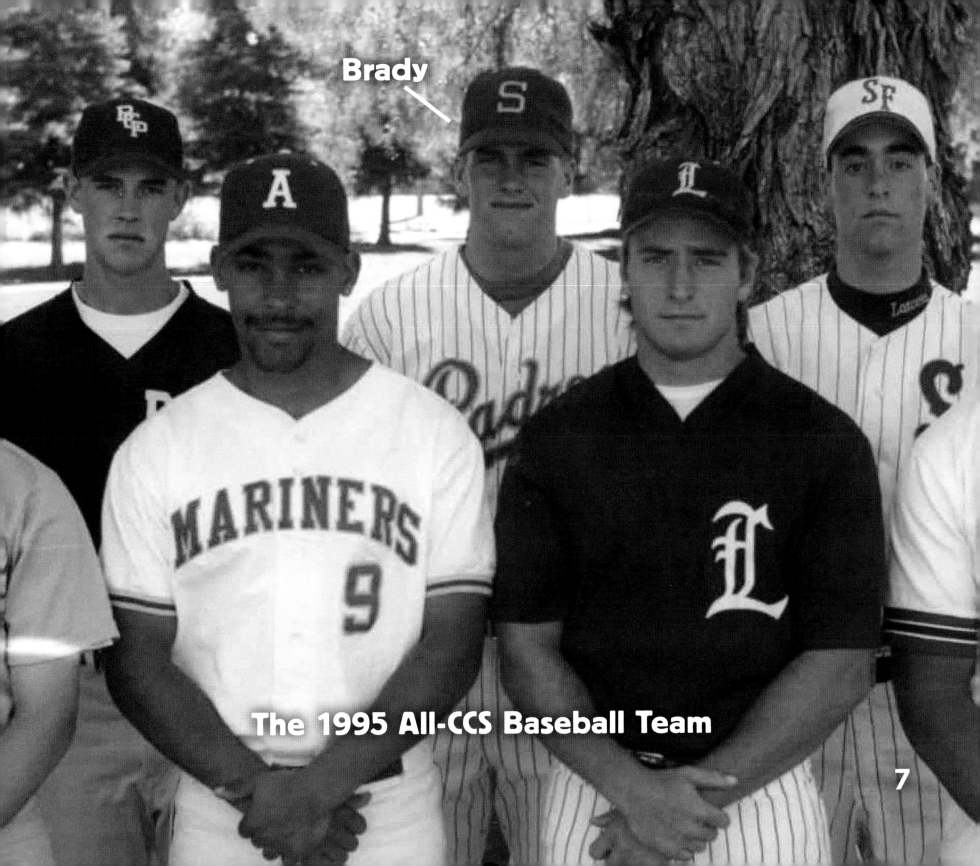

Brady

The 1995 All-CCS Baseball Team

Tom put together a **highlight reel** of his high school games. He sent it to big football colleges. The Michigan Wolverines asked Brady to play for them.

9

NFL Pro

NFL scouts did not show much interest in Brady. Some thought he was too slow. But Brady still got a call during the 2000 NFL Draft. It was from the New England Patriots.

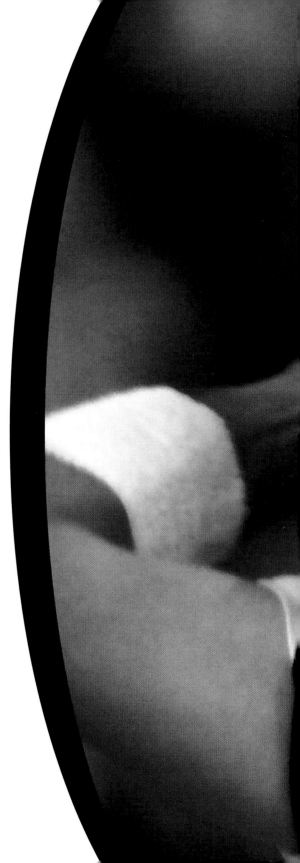

Brady rarely played in his rookie year. Then quarterback Drew Bledsoe got hurt early in the 2001 season. Brady won his first game as starting quarterback on September 30th. He ended that season as the Super Bowl MVP!

By 2005, Brady had led the Patriots to three Super Bowl wins. In the 2007 regular season, Brady threw 50 touchdown passes. And the Patriots topped it off with a perfect 16-0 record.

By 2019, Brady and the Patriots had collected three more Super Bowl rings. Then after 20 years with New England, Brady signed with the Tampa Bay Buccaneers in March of 2020.

New Team, Same Tom

The Buccaneers had some winning seasons before Brady. But the quarterback brought a whole new energy to Tampa Bay. That season, the team clinched their first **playoff berth** since 2007.

Brady then led the Buccaneers all the way to Super Bowl LV. On February 7, 2021, Tampa Bay defeated the Kansas City Chiefs 31-9. Brady was named Super Bowl MVP for a record fifth time. The NFL great is sure to excite fans for years to come.

21

Timeline

Tom graduates from high school. He goes on to attend the University of Michigan and plays QB for the Wolverines.

September 30
Brady plays and wins his first game as starting quarterback.

After 20 seasons and an incredible six Super Bowl wins with the Patriots, Brady joins the Tampa Bay Buccaneers.

1995

2001

2020

1977

2000

2002

2021

August 3
Thomas Edward Patrick Brady Jr. is born in California.

The NFL's New England Patriots pick Tom Brady in the draft. He starts his career as a fourth string QB.

Brady and the Patriots win Super Bowl XXXVI after the 2001 NFL season.

February 7
After his first season with the Buccaneers, Brady brings a Super Bowl win to Tampa Bay. It is Brady's seventh Super Bowl win.

Glossary

draft – the choosing of one or more people for sports teams.

highlight reel – the best moments caught on video in one's sports career put together to create one film.

MVP – short for "Most Valuable Player," an award given to a player who, overall, performed the best in a game or series.

playoff berth – when a position in the playoffs is secured ahead of the regular season's conclusion.

pro – short for professional.

scout – a person who looks for new sports talent.

Index

Abdo Kids
ONLINE
FREE! ONLINE MULTIMEDIA RESOURCES

Visit **abdokids.com**
to access crafts, games,
videos, and more!

Use Abdo Kids code

HHK8936

or scan this QR code!